MINKI'S
Day

Published in the United States by
QEB Publishing, Inc.
23062 La Cadena Drive
Laguna Hills, CA 92653
www.qeb-publishing.com

Library of Congress Control Number 2005921270

ISBN 1-59566-106-9

Written by Wendy Body
Designed by Alix Wood
Editor Hannah Ray
Illustrated by Sanja Rescek

Series Consultant Anne Faundez
Publisher Steve Evans
Creative Director Louise Morley
Editorial Manager Jean Coppendale

Printed and bound in China

QEB WordBanks

Learning Words with Monsters

MINKI'S
Day

Wendy Body

QEB Publishing, Inc.

At **seven o'clock**, I got up and got dressed.
I decided I wanted to look my best.

seven o'clock

5

At **eight o'clock**, still clean and neat,
breakfast was ready so I sat down to eat.

eight o'clock

At **nine o'clock**, I was in a bad mood,
my fresh clean t-shirt was splattered with food.

nine o'clock

9

At **ten o'clock**, my pet was a-quiver,
so I took him out for a walk by the river.
But I got all muddy and started to shiver
when he pulled me over and I fell in the river.

ten o'clock

At **twelve o'clock**, I was safely back home,
for lunch I had soup and my pet had a bone.

12

twelve o'clock

At **two o'clock**, it was time to help Dad.
He tried very hard, but his painting
was bad.

two o'clock

At **five o'clock**, it was time for our meal ... Mom tripped and spilled milk on me—what a big deal!

five o'clock

By **six o'clock**, I'd had enough
falling in rivers and that kind of stuff.
I'd even had milk spilled over my head,
so I jumped in the tub and then went to bed!

six o'clock

Things to do

Can you point to the times to go with the clocks?

At Minki got dressed.

At Minki ate breakfast.

At Minki went for a walk.

At Minki had lunch.

At Minki helped Dad.

At Minki's family had a meal.

five o'clock	two o'clock
seven o'clock	eight o'clock
ten o'clock	twelve o'clock

Things to do

Can you figure out how these food words begin?

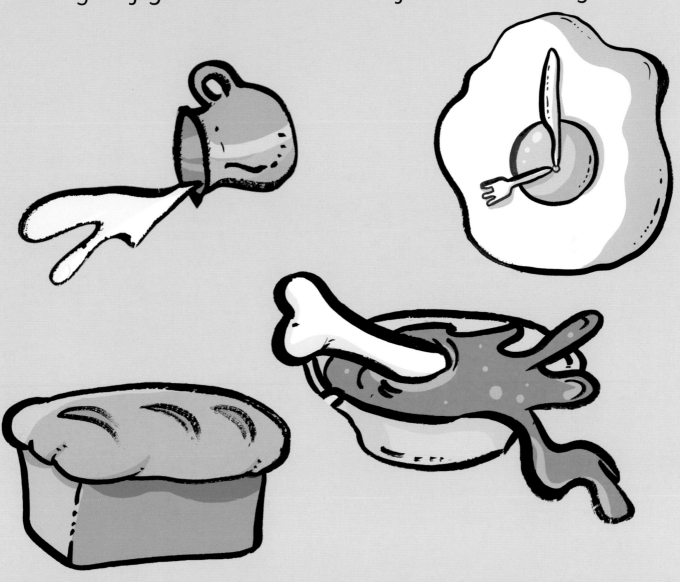

Can you think of some more food words?
How do they begin?

Word bank

Words from the story

bed
bone
breakfast
Dad
dressed
eat
food
lunch
meal
milk
Mom

o'clock
painting
pet
river
soup
t-shirt
tub

Word bank

Words about time

early	late
morning	afternoon
evening	night
yesterday	tomorrow
	today
day	week
month	year

More words about time

a quarter after
a quarter to
-thirty

a quarter after seven

a quarter to four

ten-thirty

Parents' and teachers' notes

- As you read the book to your child, run your finger along underneath the text. This will help your child to follow the reading and focus on the look of the words as well as their sound.

- The story in this book is told just as much through the illustrations as through the text, so it is essential to help your child to understand the pictures. Use open-ended questions to encourage responses, e.g. "What's happening on this page?"

- Once your child is familiar with the book, encourage him or her to join in with the reading—especially the times of the day.

- Can your child remember what Minki did at particular times of the day?

- Encourage your child to express opinions and preferences, e.g. ask questions such as, "Which picture do you think is the funniest? Why?" "Which part of the day do you think Minki disliked the most? Why?"

- Ask your child to make comparisons between Minki and themselves, e.g. "At eight o'clock, Minki ate breakfast. What time did you eat breakfast today?" Discuss what your child might do over the course of a day. Are there certain things he or she does at particular times?

- Talk about Minki's pet and think of a name for it. Encourage your child to invent and describe a monster pet of his or her own.

- Draw your child's attention to the meaning and spelling of some words, e.g. "breakfast," "lunch," "quiver," "shiver."

- Look at the "Things to do" pages (pages 20–21). Read the questions to your child and help where necessary. Give lots of encouragement. Even if your child gets something wrong, you can say, "Great try, but it's not that one. It's this one."

- Read and discuss the words on the "Word bank" pages (pages 22–23). Look at the letter patterns and how the words are spelled. Cover up the first part of a word and see if your child can remember what was there. Can your child write the simpler words from memory? Children are likely to need several attempts to write a word correctly!

- When talking about letter sounds, try not to add too much of an *uh* or *ah* sound. Say *mmm* instead of *muh* or *mah*, *ssss* instead of *suh* or *sah*. Saying letter sounds as carefully as possible will help your child when he or she is trying to build up or spell words— *huh-ah-duh* doesn't sound much like "had"!

- Talk about words: their meanings, how they sound, how they look, and how they are spelled; but if your child gets restless or bored, stop. Enjoyment of the story, activity, or book is essential if we want children to grow up valuing books and reading!